Read all the Commander in Cheese adventures!

COMMANDER IN CHEESE

Mouse Rushmore

Lindsey Leavitt
illustrated by A. G. Ford

A STEPPING STONE BOOK™

Random House 🏠 New York

Text copyright © 2017 by Lindsey Leavitt, LLC
Cover art and interior illustrations copyright © 2017 by A. G. Ford

Photo permissions pg. 105–110 president portraits, pg. 112 Mount Rushmore construction, pg. 115 Crazy Horse Memorial from the collection of Bernard Spragg at www.wikimedia.org, pg. 116 Theodore Roosevelt from the collection of the Library of Congress Prints and Photographs Division online at www.loc.gov.

Visit us on the Web!
SteppingStonesBooks.com
randomhousekids.com

Educators and librarians, for a variety of teaching tools, visit us at RHTeachersLibrarians.com

Library of Congress Cataloging-in-Publication Data is available upon request.
ISBN 978-1-5247-2047-6 (trade) — ISBN 978-1-5247-2049-0 (lib. bdg.) —
ISBN 978-1-5247-2048-3 (ebook)

Printed in the United States of America
10 9 8 7 6 5 4 3 2 1

This book has been officially leveled by using the
F&P Text Level Gradient™ Leveling System.

Random House Children's Books supports the
First Amendment and celebrates the right to read.

To the Harris crew—Ed, Anne, Kyrsti,
Devon, Brynn, and Taylor—
for kicking down signs and
breaking glass ceilings

★ ★ ★ ★ ★ ★ ★ ★ ★

Humans think they know everything about mice. Guess what. They don't.

Over the years, mice have tricked humans again and again. Mice have played dumb, sick, and even dead so humans will never know the truth: Mice are smart. Very smart. Take the smartest smart you can imagine and add two more smarts. Mice are even smarter than that.

Because mice are so smart, they let humans believe the following "facts."

(Note: These facts are NOT REALLY

TRUE. That's why there are quotation marks around "facts.")

1. **Mice don't live very long.** Mouse years are different from human years. There is a mouse in Ohio who is seventy-two. She does jumping jacks every day. Seriously.

2. **Mice are dirty.** Um . . . excuse me? Mice groom themselves. Not as often as c-a-t-s, but that's because c-a-t-s are lazy and don't do anything else all day.

3. **Mice have poor vision.** Not true! Mice have *excellent* vision. They just don't like bright lights shining in their face. Really, who does?

4. **Mice are nocturnal.** It depends on where the mice live. Take the

Squeakerton family, for example. This colony of mice has lived in the White House for over two hundred years. If the mice slept all day, they would miss out on all the presidential action.

5. **Mice don't wear clothes.** Mice are actually quite fashionable. They especially like a well-made hat. Okay, so some mice forget to wear clothes. These are also the silly mice who get caught in mousetraps.

6. **Mice don't talk to mice outside of their colony.** So untrue. Every mouse knows they can communicate using a radio. Mice in Alaska can discuss the weather with mice in Paris. Country mice and city mice have many things in common.

The Squeakertons are city mice. They are used to living in the White House, with its delicious food, warm walls, and many treasures. The Squeakertons have lived with over forty presidents. Yes, there are dangers that come from living so close to humans, but the Squeakertons like living with the Abbey family. They are nice to the mice and nice to the family c-a-t.

★ 4 ★

You can tell a lot about humans by how they treat animals.

The Squeakertons talk to country mice on the radio, but they've never actually visited farms. Or mountains. Or the desert. Or anywhere, really. Other places have just seemed less . . . cozy.

But mice are kind. They help out other mice,

no matter how different they may be. When one colony of mice is in trouble, other colonies of mice help. Sometimes this is easy to do, like running to the mouse family next door to drop off a treat.

Sometimes helping other mice is NOT easy. Sometimes it's difficult. But the Squeakertons have done difficult before.

What they haven't done before is solve a mystery.

Dean Squeakerton tossed his sister, Ava, a Frisbee made from an acorn cap. School was over for the day. Tonight their homework was to exercise for thirty minutes, read for thirty minutes, and count one hundred items in the Treasure Rooms.

Mouse school is *awesome*.

The long hallway outside their mom's office was excellent for Frisbee tossing.

"Don't throw it too hard," Dean said.

Ava flicked her wrist. The Frisbee slapped

the office door. Besides being smart, mice are also strong.

The office door creaked open. When Dean bent over to pick up the Frisbee, he heard a shaky voice coming in through the office radio.

"It's behind the faces," the voice said.

"Is there danger?" Mrs. Squeakerton asked.

Dean crouched by the door. "Ava, come here," he whispered. "Mom's talking to someone on the radio."

Mice have their own radio station for talking to mouse colonies around the world. Ava and Dean had never heard the top-secret discussions.

Until now.

"So what . . . problem?" Mrs. Squeakerton's voice was hard to hear.

Ava and Dean only heard some of the words:

". . . five treasures already lost . . ."

". . . hundreds of years of history . . ."

". . . will have to leave if this goes on . . ."

". . . not safe . . ."

Then . . . silence.

"What are they saying now?" Ava asked her brother.

Dean paused. If the voices stopped, that meant . . .

The door pulled open, and Ava and Dean flopped to the ground.

"Well, hello, little mice," Mr. Squeakerton said. "Come in. I think we need your help."

The children stepped into the office. Vivian Squeakerton was a botanist. That means she studied plants. One wall of her office was covered with pressed flowers. Another showed her plant drawings. A bookcase held seeds.

Mrs. Squeakerton spent most of her days working the dirt in the White House garden or greenhouse. She always said that Mother Nature was the greatest treasure room.

Today she had on a nice white dress and a straw hat. Ava and Dean's father, James F. Squeakerton, joined her on the couch. Gregory, a Secret Service mouse, stood behind them. Their smiles looked worried.

Ava plopped onto the lace doily that served

as a rug. "What's going on, Mom? What does *behind the faces* mean?" she asked.

"Little mice should not spy," Mrs. Squeakerton said.

"Then big mice should close the door," Dean said.

"True." Mrs. Squeakerton brushed her hands on her skirt. "We know you're friends with the president's children. We need your help."

Ava and Dean liked sharing a house with Macey and Banks. The humans and mice talked by writing things down on paper. The friendship was new, but it seemed to be working.

"I'm not giving back that Lego, if that's what you're asking." Dean sat on the couch. "Banks gave it to me."

Mr. Squeakerton laughed. "No. This is something . . . bigger. Banks and Macey are going on a trip."

Mrs. Squeakerton rubbed her daughter's head. "You see, the National Park Service gives a free pass to every fourth grader in America."

"Which is a great honor!" Gregory added.

"Yes," Mr. Squeakerton agreed. "And because Macey is in fourth grade, the First Gentleman, Dr. Abbey, is taking the kids to visit five national parks this year. Wind Cave National Park is their first one."

"Where's that?" Ava asked.

"South Dakota," Gregory said. "It's close to Mount Rushmore, a national memorial. The faces of four of our greatest presidents are carved on the stone!"

"I've always wanted to go there!" Dean said.

"Well . . . good," Mrs. Squeakerton said. "Gregory and I will come with you."

"Will we fly on Air Force One?" Ava squeaked.

"Absolutely!" Mr. Squeakerton smiled. "Now go write a note to your human friends, and we'll get ready for the trip."

Ava and Dean ran to the door. But then they stopped and looked back at their parents.

"Wait, but *why* are we going there?" Ava asked.

Mr. Squeakerton cleared his throat. "That's . . . um . . . official mouse business."

"What kind of mouse business?" Dean asked.

"Top-secret official mouse business," Mr. Squeakerton said. "Nothing for you to worry about. Run along, little mice!"

Mice are smart. Mouse kids are especially smart. Ava and Dean knew something big had happened in South Dakota. They knew it involved faces, treasure, history, and probably danger.

Most of all, they knew their parents weren't telling them everything.

"On the radio . . . when you were talking about *behind the faces,* you meant the presidents' faces," Ava said. "In the mountain."

"So we're going there. Because there's danger," Dean said. "And lost treasure."

Mr. Squeakerton shrugged. He said to his wife, "Mice are smart, honey. We need to tell them."

Mrs. Squeakerton crouched low so she was at eye level with her children. "There is a colony of country mice that live in Mount Rushmore. Their Treasure Rooms have been robbed. We need to go help them. Are you mice up for the adventure?"

Ava and Dean saluted their mom. A vacation and a chance to solve a mystery? They were in.

So in.

Ava and Dean poked their heads out from Macey's backpack. South Dakota looked bright. That might have been because they stayed in the dark backpack the entire flight. Ava wished she could see the view outside the plane, especially since she missed it when she got sick the first time she flew on Air Force One. But it *was* safer this way. Safe but not fun. Gregory's foot was in Dean's face most of the time. And now Gregory could not stop talking. He just kept shouting Mount Rushmore facts.

"Did you know it took fourteen years to carve Mount Rushmore?"

"Did you know there is a cave behind Abraham Lincoln's face called the Hall of Records?"

"Did you know the whole project cost almost a million dollars? That's like twenty million dollars today. . . ."

"No, we didn't!" Dean yelled, then took a deep breath. "We don't know anything about Mount Rushmore. We don't even know who we are meeting there. Mom, will you tell us now?"

"I don't know much myself, dear. I just know we're meeting a mouse named Mina Testerman today at three p.m." Mrs. Squeakerton ran her hand along Dean's ears. "Why don't you hop over to Macey's pocket and give her this note? Be safe, little mice."

So Ava and Dean hurried out of the backpack.

The Abbey kids stood in front of the Avenue of Flags, a long walkway displaying the state flags. Beyond that was . . .

"Whoa," Dean said.

"Mount Rushmore," Ava said.

"Whoa," Dean said again.

The blue sky stretched across Mount Rushmore. The presidential faces of George Washington, Thomas Jefferson, Theodore Roosevelt, and Abraham Lincoln looked out on the green forest. Washington's eyes even seemed to twinkle.

As amazing as it was to see the mountain, the mice didn't want anyone seeing *them*. They scurried into a mesh pocket in Macey's hiking vest.

"Hey, friends!" Macey patted her pocket. "I'm glad you can still see everything from there. It's fun having you come on this adventure with us."

"I can't believe how big this mountain is," Banks said. "The memorials in Washington, D.C., are neat, but this is huge. I wonder how long this took to create."

Dean knew Gregory was mumbling the answer from inside the backpack.

The more Dean learned about Mount Rushmore, the more it fascinated him. He wanted to be an architect when he grew up, and seeing such a large sculpture was almost as cool as seeing tall buildings.

Ava tapped Macey with a rolled-up sheet of paper. Macey read the note out loud.

Dear Macey and Banks,

Thanks for bringing us to South Dakota! We know you will see Wind Cave National Park next. You should also see the Crazy Horse Memorial.

Maybe even the bison at Custer State Park. Isn't our country cool to explore?

Before you leave, will you please drop us at the Sculptor's Studio? Don't worry. We'll stay out of trouble. We are just visiting family. Let us know when you will be back. And meanwhile, we'll get you a souvenir!

Your friends,
Ava and Dean

"How can you possibly have family in the middle of the wilderness?" Macey asked.

"Maybe all mice are family. Maybe all mice are smart," Banks said. "I mean, these mice wear clothes. We saw one dressed like Abe Lincoln. Who knows what's happening in their mouse world."

This was very clever. For a human.

Macey looked into her pocket. "Are you sure you want to stay overnight in the great outdoors? This isn't the cozy White House."

"True. There are lots of dangers outside," Banks added. "Predators, weather, avalanches . . ."

Ava and Dean had never slept outside in their life! Where were they supposed to sleep? They hadn't brought pillows. What would they eat? Country mice often ate things like berries and seeds. Did they have to gather food themselves? What about water?

Maybe the Squeakerton parents hadn't planned for this adventure.

"I would feel better about dropping you off at a building instead of on a trail," Macey said. "You are house mice."

"Yes! Our dad read us a story about that once," Banks said. " 'The City Mouse and the Country Mouse.' What happened again, Macey?"

"Didn't the mice get eaten?" Macey asked.

Ava and Dean gulped.

"No, no. They learned there is good and bad in each place," Banks said. "Something like that. Wait. Maybe only one mouse got eaten."

A man with a stiff green hat and pointy elbows shook hands with the Abbey kids. Behind him stood five Secret Service agents, three cameramen, and one press secretary. "Hi! My name is Ranger Dan. I'm taking you on a hike on the Presidential Trail. We'll head up just as soon as your father is done with the press conference."

The group waited as the First Gentleman tied his hiking boots. Then he said, "I'm so excited to tour the country, visiting different national parks, monuments, and memorials with my kids as part of my new project: See This Nation with Your Family!" He waved at the cameras. "The average parent only spends a few moments of quality time a day with their kids, but the average kid uses hours of technology. Hours! Less screen time and more family time, America."

Too bad the whole family couldn't make it. President Abbey was back at the White House. There was a crisis, but no one outside of the Situation Room knew that. Ava and Dean didn't quite know what the word *crisis* meant, but they knew the president worked hard to keep America safe.

"Let's start walking, Ranger Dan!" Dr. Abbey said.

The walk was very slow because the Abbey kids had to stop and take lots of pictures. Pictures walking along the pathway, pictures next to trees, pictures hiking up the 422 stairs. As

they walked, Ranger Dan shared facts about Mount Rushmore.

"And look! We also have beautiful wildlife at the park. Do you see that mountain goat on the cliff?"

Banks picked up his binoculars. Ava and Dean couldn't see clearly through the mesh.

Dean had been nervous since he heard the word *predators*. What did goats eat again?

"You can also see jackrabbits, mule deer, and my favorite, the Townsend's solitaire. These birds are often seen alone. And aren't the pines wonderful?"

Ava was starting to understand her mother's love of nature. The air was crisp and the sunlight warm. There was a special kind of peace and quiet that she'd never felt anywhere else.

But *this* is an adventure story. And in adventures, peace and quiet don't last very long.

"**E**xcuse me!" a man in a cowboy hat shouted. "Dr. Abbey! Dr. Abbey! We want to talk with you."

A group of humans wearing jeans, vests, and flannel shirts walked up the pathway. The Secret Service agents stood in front of the Abbey family.

"The First Gentleman is on a tour with his children," a Secret Service agent said. "He is not taking questions."

Dr. Abbey waved his hand. "It's fine. I love

talking to fellow citizens. What can I help you with?"

The man in the hat pointed at Mount Rushmore. "Last week, my friend Jamaal found a large gold nugget right here on Rushmore. Now he can quit his job at the ice cream shop and follow his dreams."

"Way to go, Jamaal!" Macey said.

"If he works at an ice cream shop, he's already living the dream," Banks said.

"We know there's gold in that hill, and we'd like the National Park Service to allow us to dig for it," the man said.

"Visitors stay on the pathways," Ranger Dan said. "Those rocks up there aren't stable! If everyone started walking and touching the monument, you'd break a leg or Jefferson's nose."

"This is a memorial, not a gold mine," Dr. Abbey agreed. "Please respect this land."

The man in the cowboy hat shrugged. "Good luck keeping people away when there's gold to be found, Dr. Abbey."

The Secret Service led the group off the path. They spoke into their walkie-talkies and discussed closing the park.

Banks groaned. "This stinks."

"Can't we go anywhere without people in suits protecting us all the time?" Macey asked. "No offense, people in suits."

"None taken," a Secret Service agent answered, his face blank.

Dr. Abbey laughed. "Let's just stop at the Sculptor's Studio, and then we'll head over to the Wind Cave. Tonight I'll make sure we do something just the three of us."

They kept walking. Stopping. Smiling. Walking. Stopping. Smiling for the camera. Ava and Dean tried not to look lumpy in the vest pocket.

Finally, they reached the Sculptor's Studio.

"Let's take a ten-minute break," Ranger Dan said. "There are some snacks and a gift shop."

Macey and Banks plopped onto a bench next to a large model of Mount Rushmore. Their dad hurried over. "Guess what! There really is an ice cream shop. We can go there right now."

Macey sat up straight. "But I want to come back tomorrow."

"Why?" Banks asked.

Macey elbowed him. Brothers can be so clueless.

"Oh, right. So we can pick up the mice," Banks said.

"Pick up the what?" Dr. Abbey asked.

"The . . . dice," Banks answered. "In the gift shop. We're . . . er . . . collecting dice now."

Ava and Dean sighed. Humans are not always as smart as mice.

Dr. Abbey grinned. "Sure. The photographers wanted to get a few more photos here tomorrow morning anyway. But first, ice cream!"

"Uh . . . sure, Dad. But we were just talking about something . . . kid stuff," Macey said. "Can you give us a second?"

Dr. Abbey held up his hands. "You guys want to bond. I get it."

"Dads can be so weird sometimes," Banks whispered.

Once Dr. Abbey was gone, Ava and Dean climbed out of the pocket and into Macey's cupped hand. Gregory and Mrs. Squeakerton scurried out of the backpack and through a cracked-open door.

"Are you sure you don't want to stay, little

mice?" Macey asked. "You can see more sights with us."

Of course Ava would rather have stayed in a cozy hotel room with Macey. But the mice were here for a reason, even if she didn't completely know the reason yet. She pointed to the staff room door that her mom and Gregory had gone through. Macey carried them over to the doorway.

"We'll come back for you tomorrow at ten a.m.," Macey said. "Make sure you're here on time. We won't be able to wait for you."

"Have fun exploring!" Banks said. "Be safe!"

Ava and Dean ran into the dark room. Mrs. Squeakerton and Gregory waited for them near a mouse hole hidden behind a vending machine.

Mrs. Squeakerton took her kids' claws.

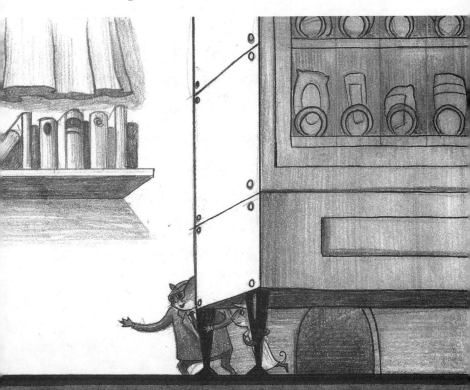

"Good job, little mice! You got us here. Now let's see what these country mice need."

The Squeakertons entered a dark tunnel with a dirt floor. Ava ran her claw along the smooth walls. The tunnel ended in a small cave.

A mouse waited in front of a door.

"Oh, good. You made it. I'm Mina Testerman." Mina wore a fringed tan dress with blue beading around the collar. Her accent was different from the Squeakerton mice's. Ava and Dean had only ever spoken to Washington, D.C., mice. They had never used the radio. They had never before heard an accent. "We are so glad you were able to help us. Thank you for traveling such a great distance."

"We are excited to see your little mouse burrows," Gregory said. "I've read about mice who live in the wild. It's quite different from our fancy White House life."

"Oh, I'm sure it's wonderful living in the president's house." Mina smiled warmly. "Instead, we just live inside the president's head. Actually, a little above Lincoln's chin."

"Well, he had quite the chin," Gregory said.

"Are you a big fan of presidents?" Mina asked.

"The biggest!" Gregory said. "Aren't you?"

"Not especially," Mina said. "Although it's not the presidents' fault that their faces got carved onto our mountain, is it?" Mina pushed a button, and the doors slid open.

"Is this . . . You have an elevator?" Gregory asked.

"We call it a slide-o-vator. Sort of like a train, I suppose. It moves in all directions," Mina said. "Please, join me."

The Squeakertons stepped into the slide-o-vator. When the doors closed, the box pushed to the right.

"Whoa," Ava said. "Who invented this?"

"My ancestor," Mina said. "Back when they started carving the faces, in 1927. We figured we should have a hole in the studio so we could learn what the silly humans were up to."

The slide-o-vator lurched forward. Yes, forward. Then it rolled up, down, and sideways. The Squeakertons grabbed the railing. Mina stayed calm and still.

"I will quickly show you our burrow," Mina said.

"How far away is it?" Dean asked.

"About a human mile. We should arrive . . ." The slide-o-vator stopped, and the doors slid open. "Now."

The Squeakertons walked into the biggest room they had ever seen. And these were mice that had watched state dinners in the White House East Room. They knew big.

"It's bigger than a football field," Dean said in wonder.

"It's like New York City," Ava said. "For mice."

It was hard for the Squeakertons to see all the details in the dim light. They could see streets, homes, and other buildings made out of everything from brick to stone to clay. There looked to be a park to their right and a café to their left. The only light in the room came from a hole cut in the ceiling.

"Do you have a flashlight?" Gregory asked.

"Oh, yes. You must be used to human electrical lighting." Mina handed each mouse a headlamp. "We light the streetlamps at night, but we mostly use our whiskers for direction."

Dean rubbed his whiskers. He had never really thought to *use* them for anything. "Where is everyone?" he asked.

"Asleep. It's daytime." Mina laughed. "I almost forgot—you aren't nocturnal! I remember your dad told a funny story on his radio show. You got up in the middle of the night for water and ran into Woodrow Wilson's shoehorn! A mouse that can't see in the dark? We laughed forever."

Ava and Dean wished their dad would share

less embarrassing family stories on his radio broadcast. They knew they were sorta famous, for mice. It was weird having someone they had just met already know things about them.

"Well, life is different in the White House," Dean said defensively.

"Can you tell us more about this room?" Mrs. Squeakerton asked kindly.

"Yes. Hold hands and follow me." Mina led them down six mouse blocks. They passed streetlamps, mouse mailboxes, and even mini trees. Mina stopped in front of a statue of a mouse. His leg was up on a boulder. He had a bow and arrows on his back, and a fierce mousy look in his eyes.

"This is Chief Standing Mouse. The statue is the town meeting place. We meet here at sunset for a group hug and at sunrise for a tribe meeting," Mina said.

"How many mice meet here?" Ava asked.

"Well, let's see." Mina rubbed her chin. "We've welcomed new mice here for generations. We are careful to avoid predators. So I'd say there are probably twenty thousand mice living here."

Ava wasn't sure how many Squeakertons lived in the White House, but she knew the number was in the hundreds, not the thousands.

"There are many more rooms cut from our main burrow." Mina pointed to some tunnels. "I believe our ancestors started this burrow about five hundred years ago."

Gregory's mouth hung open. "But Mount Rushmore isn't even a hundred years old."

"There were mice before Mount Rushmore," Mina said. "There were humans before Mount Rushmore. The Lakota people lived in the

Black Hills for hundreds of years. They called this mountain the Six Grandfathers. We lived in harmony with the original humans."

"And now?" Gregory asked.

"Now . . . we have a problem," Mina said worriedly. "We believe we've been discovered. Follow me to the Treasure Rooms."

The Testerman Treasure Rooms were triple the size of the Squeakertons'. There were rooms and rooms of odds and ends.

"This is the Arrowhead Collection," Mina said. "Behind that is the Tools Collection. We have a Twigs Collection and a Lost Cameras Collection. Oh, and a Candy Collection."

Dean's ears pointed. "A Candy Collection?"

Mina nodded. "Mount Rushmore gets three million visitors a year. Kids have been leaving candy forever. I wouldn't eat any of it."

"But sugar is sugar." Dean sighed. "Do you have a *Fresh* Candy Collection? I love those chocolate gold coins."

"Well, if it's gold coins you want, come in here."

And that's when the Squeakertons walked into the Expensive Stuff Collection. There weren't buttons or toys or candy in this room. This was real live *treasure*.

"There has to be thousands of dollars of gold in here," Mrs. Squeakerton said.

Mina smiled. "Millions. And millions. And millions."

Gregory admired a sword. "Is this real gold?"

"That was from a Civil War soldier. There's still blood on it."

Gregory backed away slowly.

"How can you even tell that anything is missing?" Ava asked.

Mina pulled out a tablet. She pushed a button, and a list appeared on the screen. "We do a daily inventory of all our items. Don't you do that at the White House?"

"Uh . . . no," Mrs. Squeakerton said. The Squeakerton mice didn't have that kind of technology. Plus, they weren't worried about anyone taking their treasure. No one knew they were there.

Mina shrugged. "Well, we've noticed small items disappearing over the last week. First, it was a rug. Then a scarf. Some branches from rare plants. But the last item was a large gold nugget." Mina set down her tablet. "These aren't just a few lost objects. We have a thief."

Gregory leaned against a silver watch. "So . . . who do you think did it?"

"There are two openings to the Treasure Rooms. A computer scans your claw at the main entrance. Only Treasure Keepers can enter alone, but any Testerman mouse can visit. We have everything we need, so I don't think a mouse would steal."

"Where is the other opening?" Ava asked.

"At the back of the Hall of Records. The Hall of Records is a cave behind Abraham Lincoln's face. The sculptor Gutzon Borglum wanted to store important US documents there. Of course, they were getting close to our burrow, so we put a stop to that."

"I thought the US government put a stop to that," Gregory said.

Mina winked. "We created a rockslide to scare them into stopping. Mice are smart."

"Maybe it's a ghost?" Dean said, excited. "I've wanted to see a ghost forever. Our great-great-grandpa swore he saw Rutherford B. Hayes playing pool in the Game Room."

"What would a ghost want with a mouse rug?" Gregory asked.

"Could it be something in nature?" Mrs. Squeakerton asked. "Like . . . wind?"

"But the wind would blow everything," Mina reasoned. "Not just some things."

"Humans know about the hall because they built it," Ava said. "So maybe one got up here."

"It would be very hard for a human to get

up here without security noticing," Mina said. "Humans built a time capsule in 1998. That's the last time we saw a human nearby."

The mice thought. They wondered. They considered.

Dean jumped up. "Hey! The treasure hunters! Someone found gold here last week, and now they all want to dig up Rushmore."

Mina looked alarmed. "They can't do that! We have worked very hard to keep our burrow a secret from humans. Stolen treasure is one thing. Humans discovering a huge ancient mouse city is another. These thieves could ruin our burrow."

"I have an idea." Ava hopped onto a gold bison figurine. "We can stop the humans right now."

"How?" Gregory asked.

"We know who the thief is," Ava said.

"That's right." Dean pumped his fist in the air. "The guy who works at the ice cream shop found a gold nugget."

"You mean *stole* a gold nugget," Mina said.

"What was his name?" Dean asked. "Jared? Jack? James?"

"Jamaal," Ava said. "We have our guy."

"Well done!" Mina clapped.

"But . . . ," Gregory said, plopping down next to a large ruby, "we're talking about a full-grown human here. How on earth are we going to *get* this guy?"

Ava and Dean smiled at each other. "That's the fun part."

The Squeakertons' Human-Catching List

1. Glasses
2. Marbles
3. Shiny gold ring
4. Raspberries
5. Toothpaste
6. Cymbals
7. Prickly thorns
8. Beeswax
9. Rope
10. More rope

"How are we going to use this?" Gregory held up a raspberry.

"Those are snacks for later." Dean shoved more berries into his backpack. He would have preferred cheese, maybe a nice Gouda, but the Testermans didn't have cheese.

They walked outside. There was a tram built into the mountain. Mina hopped into the cart. "Buckle your seat belts."

The Squeakertons couldn't see their seat belts, or anything really. The sun had already set. They switched on their headlamps.

A coyote howled. Dean jumped. "What about . . . what about predators?"

"Mice always have to worry about predators," Mina said. "I mean, I guess you don't. In the White House."

"Tell that to the mice who lived with President Jimmy Carter!" Gregory boomed. "He found a mouse in the Oval Office in 1978 and set enough traps to kill dozens of us. Horrible tragedy."

"We don't have a lot of Jimmy Carter's stuff in the Treasure Rooms," Mrs. Squeakerton said quietly.

The chirping of a bird drowned out the coyote's howls. "Don't worry, that's not a bird of prey," Mina said. "Sounds like a thrush. Must have a new nest built up high. Been hearing that chirping for weeks. Chirp, chirp, chirp. Wish birds were as smart as mice."

"Isn't that the truth?" Dean laughed.

"I wish we were closer so we could understand the bird," Mrs. Squeakerton said.

"The bird could eat us!" Ava said. "No way am I getting close to any animals out here."

"Well, hold on to your headlamps," Mina said. "We have a booby trap to set!"

The cart rolled down the tracks. It picked up speed and twisted around the side of the mountain.

"This . . . this is like a roller coaster." Mrs. Squeakerton's teeth chattered.

"Of course it is!" Mina threw her arms in the air. "We have a slide-o-vator already. This tram was built for *fun*!"

The mice flew down the mountain, dipping around boulders and swooping under trees. Dean felt like he was flying! Ava felt like she might throw up. Motion sickness stinks.

Finally, the track rolled into a straight road, and the cart swerved to a stop.

"The Memorial Team Ice Cream shop is in the granite buildings by the flags." Mina slung a pack over her shoulder. "Come along!"

The shop was named after the baseball team formed by the carvers of Mount Rushmore.

Some of the men who carved the mountain were hired for their baseball skills instead of their sculpting.

"'This team played in the 1939 state championship,'" Dean read from a plaque. "They had

a chance to carve a mountain every day. Why
waste time playing baseball?"

"Dean!" Gregory hissed. "This is not the
time to read historical facts."

Not the time to read historical facts? When

had Gregory ever said such a thing? Clearly, he was taking this human trapping very seriously.

"There's Jamaal." Ava pointed at a bald man wiping down the counter.

"How can you tell?" Mrs. Squeakerton asked.

"His name tag," Ava said.

"Let's go set up," Dean said.

The mice snuck into the back room.

Ava and Dean quietly set out the marbles, one by one.

Mrs. Squeakerton shoved the thorns into a blow dart. (Oh, that wasn't on the list! Yes, there was also a blow dart. Surprise!)

Gregory shined the ring until it sparkled.

Mina unraveled the rope.

The mice waited for two minutes. They waited for twenty minutes. Still no Jamaal. All they needed was for him to walk into the room.

Then the toothpaste would squirt out, the marbles would roll, and the glasses would . . .

Look, it was a smart plan. If you're a mouse, you probably already see where this plan is going. If you're a human, you probably wouldn't understand even if someone explained it to you.

Either way, the plan wouldn't work if Jamaal didn't walk into the room!

"Use the cymbals," Mrs. Squeakerton whispered.

"If this doesn't work, I can run up his pant leg," Gregory said. "I'll grab him by the neck in a secret hold that will make him fall over. We'll call about five hundred—no, probably a thousand mice down to drag him back up the mountain. Then we'll squirt hot sauce up his nose until he tells the truth—"

"We are peaceful mice!" Mina interrupted.

"Oh. Yeah. So are we," Gregory said. "Okay. We'll try this first."

Gregory stuck some beeswax into his ears. The other mice covered their own ears. Gregory clashed the cymbals together.

"What was that?" Jamaal ran into the dark room.

"Jamaal?" someone called out.

"Did you hear that?" He reached for the light switch.

"Hear what? Come talk to me."

Jamaal shrugged and shut the door.

"Are you *kidding* me?" Gregory asked.

"There's no way that guy is smart enough to be the treasure thief!" Ava said. "We could be back here robbing him, and he would just let us."

"I guess we try plan B," Dean said.

"What's that?" Mina asked.

"We spy," Dean answered. "Now stay quiet as a mouse."

The Squeakertons ran underneath the ice cream counter.

"Annie!" Jamaal walked around the counter and gave a lady a hug. "So glad you came in. It's my last night working."

"What were you doing in the back room?" Annie asked.

"Thought I heard something." Jamaal opened the ice cream fridge. "Have a seat. This one is on the house."

Jamaal whistled as he scooped ice cream. The mice could only see his feet, but there was definitely a skip in his step.

"Let's see how happy this guy is once we send him to jail," Gregory said.

"I heard you found some gold up the mountain." Annie sat on a counter stool.

"Yes, ma'am. Size of a golf ball," Jamaal

said. "Bought an RV with the money. I'm going to tour the country."

"I've been working as a ranger here for thirty years." Annie drummed her fingers. "Never seen or heard of any gold."

"Me neither," Jamaal said. He gave Annie a banana split.

"Then how in the world did you find that?" Annie asked.

Jamaal was quiet for a bit. The Squeakertons made sure they listened really, really closely.

Jamaal waited until the other customers left. Then he leaned across the counter and said, "The nugget . . . landed in my lap."

"Breaking into a Treasure Room is not exactly having something land in your lap," Gregory scoffed.

"Shhh," Mrs. Squeakerton said.

"I was doing my morning walk along the Presidential Trail," Jamaal said. "Four times, so it's about two and a half miles. I was by the close part, kind of under Washington's nose with that big boulder. Then I heard this shuffle. Rocks slid down the side. The gold sparkled in the light. I picked it right up."

"Sounds like Lady Luck wanted you to have that gold." Annie took a bite of ice cream.

"Someone did." Jamaal shrugged.

"Don't you think we should climb up closer to the faces and see if there's any more gold up there?" Annie asked.

"When luck happens like that, you don't ask too many questions. One nugget is plenty for me." Jamaal looked at his watch. "It's about closing time. I'll walk you out."

The mice waited for the doorbells to chime before scurrying to the back room. They grabbed what they could of the supplies. They didn't need a booby trap anymore.

"Do you think he's telling the truth?" Mrs. Squeakerton asked.

Mina scratched her head. "When Ava said someone 'found' gold, it made sense that Jamaal had taken our missing gold. But now I'm not sure. For a human to get to the Hall of Records, they need to climb up the mountain. There are thousands of tourists during the day, and the mountain is lit up at night."

"So someone would see him," Ava said.

"Yes." Mina nodded. "And another thing . . . the opening to our Treasure Rooms is the size of a bowling ball. The human couldn't get in, not unless they sent some robbing robot in there."

"Jamaal doesn't seem like the type of guy to own a robot," Dean said.

"Exactly." Mina rubbed her whiskers. "The

problem isn't that someone took the treasure. We have plenty of treasure. Besides, we took lots of those items from humans in the first place."

"Oh. Yeah." Gregory's face reddened. "I guess in that case, we're all kind of thieves."

"Borrowers," Mina corrected. "What worries me is that someone—something—knows the Treasure Rooms exist. If it's not a mouse taking things, then our burrow is in danger. And if it *is* a mouse taking things, well . . ."

"Then it looks like our thief lives much closer than we thought," Gregory said.

Mina seemed upset as they rode the slide-o-vator back up the mountain. Ava and Dean could understand—they would feel the same way if there was a mess like this in the White House.

"I still don't understand how the gold nugget went from our Treasure Rooms to landing at Jamaal's feet." Mina sighed.

It was very dark outside. It was very dark inside. It was very late, and Ava was tired. "What time is it?"

"Midnight." Mrs. Squeakerton hugged her

daughter. "We should go to bed. We'll figure out the rest in the morning."

Mina smiled. "It already is morning for us. You can say hello to everyone before bedtime. Morning time. Whatever."

Ava and Dean walked out to the largest gathering of mice they'd ever seen. Thousands and thousands of Testerman mice filled the town square. They wore clothes from all different periods of time. Some even wore clothes that looked like they were from the future. The town hummed with activity.

"I'm starting to feel like we're the country mice here," Dean whispered to his sister.

A mouse in a purple suit ran up to Mina. "Did you . . . figure out the problem yet?"

Mina smiled at the Squeakertons. "This is Mato."

Mato nodded at them before turning back to Mina. "Did they help you? Is it fixed?"

"We haven't told anyone about the missing items," Mina said quietly to the Squeakertons. "We didn't want anyone to panic."

"I'm panicking!" Mato said. "I just did the last shift. This makes no sense. None!"

"Shift?" Ava asked.

"We started taking turns in the Treasure Rooms," Mina explained. "Kind of like a stake-out. In case anyone tries to steal again."

"We want to do the next shift!" Dean jumped up. "Come on, Ava."

"I thought you little mice said you were tired," Mrs. Squeakerton said.

"We'll take turns sleeping." Ava grabbed her brother's tail. "We can't quit now, not when we're so close to solving the mystery."

"Well, I'm going to bed," Mrs. Squeakerton said.

"That's fine," Dean said. "Let's go, Gregory."

"'Let's go, Gregory'?" Gregory repeated. "Why can't I go to bed too?"

"Because *we* aren't," Ava said. "And you have to watch us."

"It would be great if you could help us!" Mina said. "Only four Treasure Keepers know about the missing treasure, and their watch is over." She scanned her claw on a keypad to open the door to the Treasure Rooms. "We'll need someone by the hole and someone by the entrance."

"And someone in the Candy Collection?" Dean asked hopefully.

"I think the Candy Collection is fine on its own." Mina smiled. "Are you sure you'll be okay in here?"

Ava gave a thumbs-up. Well, a claws-up.

"Gregory, you watch the door," Ava said. "We'll watch the hole."

Ava and Dean ran through rooms until they reached the Expensive Stuff Collection. They made chairs out of gold goblets. They used scarves for blankets. But . . . it turns out watching a hole is not as exciting as it sounds.

"So what happens next?" Dean asked.

"We wait and see if something or someone comes through that hole," Ava said. "Then I guess one of us runs to get Mina."

"What does the other person do?" Dean asked.

"I don't know. Fight? There's a sword you can use," Ava said.

Dean gulped.

For the next few hours, Ava and Dean took turns dozing off. When they were awake, they paced the Treasure Rooms or counted the gold. At 8:00 a.m., their shift was close to ending, and still . . . nothing.

They'd come all this way to help, and now the Testerman mice weren't any closer to figuring out who was stealing from the Treasure Rooms. And if someone *kept* stealing, then what would the Testermans do? Leave?

"This isn't a stakeout! It's a fakeout." Dean kicked at a rock on the ground. The rock bounced against the cave wall. And then . . . the room shook. Large rocks fell from the stony ceiling. The mice ducked and covered their heads.

"Did I do that?" Dean asked.

The room shook again. Dirt swirled in the air.

Ava squeaked. "I'll get Gregory."

"No, I'll get Gregory."

"Dean, *stay*!"

Ava ran through the Treasure Rooms to the main entrance. Gregory's head was on a table. He snorted a snore that woke him up. "Did you know Ronald Reagan loved jelly beans? Wait, where am I?"

"Gregory! There's something happening! Sound the alarm and follow me."

Gregory slapped the emergency alarm with

his claw. They hurried back to Dean, who stood shaking in front of the mouse hole.

"I liked this stakeout better when nothing was happening," Dean whispered.

There was a faint crunching sound, then voices.

Human voices.

"Okay, this is what we'll do." Ranger Dan's voice rang through the Hall of Records. The voice was still far but not far enough. "Let's run our metal detectors across the mountain. Be gentle around the presidents' faces. Don't touch."

"What happens when we don't find any gold?" someone asked.

"Then we release this video to prove there isn't gold up here. We've had three gold hunters sneak off the trail tonight already. We need to protect Mount Rushmore."

"What happens if we *do* find gold?" some-one else asked.

"Then you tell me," Ranger Dan said. "Immediately."

Mina rushed into the Treasure Rooms, fol-lowed by Mrs. Squeakerton and a handful of other mice. "Is it humans?" she whispered.

Ava and Dean nodded. It was silent in the

Hall of Records. The silence was interrupted by quick beeps, which got longer and closer.

"What is that beeping?" Dean asked.

"Metal detectors," Mina moaned. "If they bring those things into the Hall of Records, they'll beep right by Treasure Rooms. Out there, they would have to dig really deep to get to our burrow. But right here . . . we'll be found. We need to get everyone out of the burrow. Now!"

"But . . . but what about the hole?" Mrs. Squeakerton asked. "How do you cover up the hole?"

"There's a stone. But it needs to be moved from the outside. So whoever did it would—"

"Be stuck in the Hall of Records with humans," Gregory finished. "But if we don't do it, we're all going to be found anyway."

The beeping of the metal detectors was getting louder. Closer.

"It's too dangerous," Mina said. "We asked for your help, but not this kind of help. Please, let's run now."

" 'We must dare to be great; and we must realize that greatness is the fruit of toil and sacrifice and high courage.' Teddy Roosevelt said that, and I believe it." Gregory saluted the other mice.

"Yeah, what Gregory said." Ava and Dean stood tall by their brave bodyguard.

"No!" Mrs. Squeakerton said. "Absolutely not. You little mice are staying with me. It's safer that way."

"If we get caught, then Dean and I can give a note to Ranger Dan," Ava said. "He'll get it back to Macey."

"Unless he steps on you first," Mrs. Squeakerton said.

"Unless he steps on us first," Dean agreed.

"But, Mom, we can make it back in time. This is the only way. If we stay in the burrow, we'll never make it down to the Sculptor's Studio in time for the Abbeys' departure."

Mrs. Squeakerton nodded. "So either we leave now, or we never leave South Dakota."

Mina hugged each Squeakerton. "Thank you for doing this. Please take a treasure with you. Any item you like."

"Well, if you insist," Gregory said, running immediately to grab Calvin Coolidge's gold cuff links.

Mrs. Squeakerton shook her head. "This much fresh air was treasure enough for me. Ava? Dean? What would you like?"

"I'm taking this jewelry." Ava held up a gold-and-emerald brooch shaped like a c-a-t. "It's very unique."

"I already got mine." Dean held up a butterscotch.

"Really?" Ava asked. "There are precious jewels right behind you, and you pick candy?"

"Butterscotch lasts for years!" Dean said. "It probably still tastes good. Emeralds taste horrible."

The mice stuffed their treasures into their packs and stepped out of the room.

This is the bad news for the Squeakertons:

1. They might get stuck in the cave forever.
2. They might get caught by humans.
3. Predators might kill them once they leave the cave.
4. They might slip on the granite rocks.
5. They might miss the Abbey kids and have to stay in South Dakota forever.

This is the better news:

1. They were still alive.
2. Dean had candy they could eat if they got hungry.
3. They'd seen more nature in one day than they had their entire lives in the White House.
4. They were helping their new friend, Mina.
5. And . . . that's it. Not the best list.

Mina waved. "Be brave, mice!" she called before running out of the Treasure Rooms. She needed to guide the other Testerman mice through the emergency tunnels that led to a far-away meadow.

Mrs. Squeakerton, Gregory, Dean, and Ava

joined hands. The beeping was now right outside the tunnel.

"Well, let's move a stone!" Gregory said.

"Hey, what's this on the ground?" Ava picked up a feather. "Did this blow out of the Treasure Rooms?"

"Probably," Dean said. "Put it down and come help."

Mice are strong, but stones aren't exactly

light. It took all four mice pushing and grunting before the stone would even budge. It slowly rolled until it covered the hole in the wall.

And just in time.

The humans were now in the Hall of Records.

8

"We're just going to walk through the hall." Ranger Dan's voice rang through the dark cave.

The Squeakertons crouched in the corner.

"I've been waiting to come into this hall for years," a female voice said.

"Me too, Ranger Lyla." Ranger Dan whistled as he walked around the large space. "You know, they could make a lot of money if they let tourists in here. Charge an entrance fee."

"That wouldn't be good for the sculpture. Too much foot traffic," Ranger Lyla said.

"If we find gold, we can quit being rangers and buy a house together in Australia," Ranger Dan said.

"Dan, we just started dating," Ranger Lyla said. "How many times do I have to tell you? I'm not moving to Australia."

The rangers continued to scan the space. The Squeakertons tried to look small. They tried to look invisible. But it didn't work.

Ranger Dan waved his metal detector over the mice.

It beeped because of the gold cuff links Gregory had picked out. Which was not the smartest mouse moment.

"There is gold in Rushmore! And now it will be mine, and no one else will ever have to know." Ranger Dan felt around in the darkness.

"You mean it will be *ours*," Ranger Lyla said. "Right?"

Gregory was tempted to bite Ranger Dan. He'd seemed like such a nice guy back on the trail. Money makes humans do stupid things.

"Scurry," Mrs. Squeakerton whispered. "Now."

Ava made it past Ranger Dan. Dean made it past Ranger Dan. Mrs. Squeakerton made it past Ranger Dan.

Gregory did not make it past Ranger Dan.

But for once, Gregory was very glad that he was often mistaken for other species.

"It's a rat!" Ranger Dan squealed. "Oh, Lyla, I *hate* rats."

He dropped Gregory, but Lyla just swooped him right back up. She looked closely at Gregory. "He's bigger than that. Maybe . . . a possum? Did you run the metal detector over him, or did it ring in the corner?"

"If there's one rat in here, there could be hundreds!" Ranger Dan yelped. "I hate animals! Smash it!"

Ranger Lyla waved her detector over Gregory. It beeped again. "Do you think this guy swallowed some metal? He keeps beeping."

Ranger Dan started fumbling around the floor, maybe looking for a rock. Gregory did not want to find out what he was looking for. He tried to hop down, but Ranger Lyla had a strong grip.

Just then, a bird started chirping.

"And birds? This hall has been taken over by animals." Ranger Dan was close to tears. "Come on, Lyla. The detector didn't beep anywhere else in here. There's no gold. That dumb animal probably just swallowed a dime."

Dumb animal? Gregory really wanted to correct Ranger Dan.

Lyla sighed. "Shouldn't we look a little more? I mean, of course there are animals in here. It's a cave in a mountain. Perfect habitat."

The chirping turned into squawking. The sound echoed against the walls. The Squeakertons picked up the hint and started making squeaking sounds. The cave sounded like it was filled with dozens of living creatures.

"We're going to get a disease from these animals! I'm leaving." Dan ran out of the Hall of Records, screaming.

Lyla slid Gregory back to the floor. "If the

man hates animals, what is he doing being a park ranger? And what does he think Australia has? There are sharks! Snakes! Spiders!"

She shook her head and wandered outside.

"No gold in there," Ranger Dan huffed to the other searchers. "Did anyone else find anything?"

"Not one beep."

"Nothing."

"All we found was a gerbil who maybe had a gold tooth," Ranger Lyla said. "And it was dark, but I think he was wearing a suit."

"You saw his tooth?" Ranger Dan asked.

"It was a joke, Dan. Let's get you back to the Sculptor's Studio. Get you an aspirin and a nap."

Finally, the humans climbed back down the side of the mountain. The mice were left alone. Sort of.

"Stay close to the wall, little mice," Gregory called.

The bird chirped again. This chirp seemed friendly.

"We still have a visitor in here, and I want to figure out who it is." Mrs. Squeakerton cleared her throat. Then she chirped.

Some animals are able to speak a language of other animals. Apparently, Mrs. Squeakerton could speak Bird.

The bird chirped back. Mrs. Squeakerton chirped again.

"This bird is a friend. Come along," Mrs. Squeakerton said.

"How did you learn to do that?" Ava asked, amazed.

"Working in the garden. We help each other find what we need—seeds, worms, whatever. And this bird . . . she needs some help."

At the edge of the tunnel waited a round brown bird that was not much bigger than Gregory.

Mrs. Squeakerton stepped forward. She carefully ran her hand along the bird's wing.

"She's hurt," she said. "She broke her wing two weeks ago and couldn't fly anywhere to get food for her babies. She hopped into the Treasure Rooms so she could find a few items for her nest. She said she took some of the candy too. I guess the Testermans didn't notice that."

"I should have taken more candy!" Dean said under his breath.

The bird chirped again. "She tried to talk to the mice, but the sword in the Expensive Stuff Collection scared her off. She thought the mice might hurt her. So she took the gold nugget and threw it down the mountain."

"That makes no sense," Gregory said.

"Yes, it does," Mrs. Squeakerton said. "It got Jamaal's attention. It got ours. She just wanted someone to come up and help her with her babies until she could fly again."

"Well, mystery solved!" Gregory brushed off his suit. "Now let's head back to the Sculptor's Studio so we can find the Abbey children and go home."

Ava rolled her eyes. "Gregory, we have to help her!"

Gregory moaned. "But she almost got us killed!"

"And then she saved us," Dean said. "Mom, ask the bird her name."

Mrs. Squeakerton chirped. The bird chirped.

"Her name is Zitkala. She's a Townsend's solitaire. Let's go see her nest."

"Where is it?" Gregory asked.

"In Theodore Roosevelt's mustache," Mrs. Squeakerton said.

9

There were lots of things the Squeakerton mice had never thought they would do, like:

1. Leave the White House
2. Set a booby trap
3. Meet a huge colony of South Dakotan mice
4. Solve a mystery
5. Climb a mountain

"What if I fall?" Gregory asked as he very, very carefully climbed the rocks.

"What if you fly?" Ava asked.

"That makes no sense," Gregory said.

"Maybe," Ava said. "But look. We made it to the mustache."

Teddy Roosevelt did have a very full mustache. It was an excellent perch for Zitkala's nest.

The chicks chirped to their mother. Zitkala chirped to Mrs. Squeakerton.

"She says her chicks are very hungry. We could get her food from the Treasure Rooms, but what if the humans come back in? Or we can't move the stone?"

Dean sighed. "Fine. They can have my butterscotch."

"One butterscotch isn't going to do much."

"I might have borrowed more than one," Dean said. He reached into his backpack and pulled out two candies. He also pulled

out the raspberries left over from the Jamaal
adventure.

"How did you pack so much in there?" Gregory asked.

"I take food very seriously," Dean said.

"The raspberries will be much better for the birds than butterscotch," Gregory said. "Keep the candy."

"Yes, sir!" Dean saluted Gregory.

"The berries are enough for right now, but Zitkala will need to find another way to get food," Mrs. Squeakerton said.

Gregory squinted at the sun. "What time is it?"

Mrs. Squeakerton squeaked. "I didn't even think about that! It's got to be close to nine. We need to meet the Abbey children at ten o'clock."

"Can Zitkala come with us?" Ava asked. "Just to the studio. We can write a note, and she can take it back to the Testermans in the slide-o-vator. They'll help her once they know what happened."

"Excellent idea!" Gregory peered over the mustache. "Now how are we going to get down?"

Mrs. Squeakerton smiled. "They don't call them *rock-slides* for nothing."

So the Squeakerton mice and Zitkala slid down the side of Theodore Roosevelt's face. They scurried to a tree underneath Thomas Jefferson. The tram was still there.

"How are we going to fit?" Dean asked. Zitkala wasn't a big bird, but she wasn't exactly small either.

"Squeeze," Mrs. Squeakerton said. "And hurry. We might be too late already."

Four mice and one bird stuffed themselves into the cart. This ride down the mountain was not quite as fun as last time. Worrying about catching a flight can be very stressful, even for mice.

"I wish we could go back ourselves and tell Mina what happened," Dean said.

"So she can help Zitkala? Me too," Ava said.

"No, so we can get credit for solving the

mystery." Dean sighed. "Being a detective is hard work."

The tram lurched to a stop.

"Run, little mice!" Mrs. Squeakerton said. "Run like you've never run before."

Gregory carried Zitkala on his back. Mice are so strong.

After more running, hiding, scurrying, and hurrying, the group made it to the Sculptor's Studio. The Abbey kids were already being photographed in front of the Rushmore model.

"We did it!" Dean huffed.

"Yay! I'll just write a note explaining everything." Ava pulled out a piece of paper from her pack. "Wait, I don't have a pencil. How will the Testermans know Zitkala was with us and needs help?"

So close! The plan was almost perfect, but now Zitkala wouldn't be able to get help from the Testermans. She was still in trouble.

"Give her these." Gregory held out the cuff links to Zitkala. "Then they'll know you were with us."

"But, Gregory!" Mrs. Squeakerton said.

Gregory looked away. One tear slipped down his cheek. "Calvin Coolidge went fishing in South Dakota and loved it. That's how Mount Rushmore got its funding. It was worth it to . . . understand how Calvin felt."

"Keep one cuff link," Ava said. "They don't need both."

Now more tears spilled down Gregory's face, but they were tears of joy.

That mouse really loves presidents.

Zitkala chirped quickly.

Mrs. Squeakerton patted her good wing. "She says thank you."

Dean grabbed a stick and scratched on the paper, *Bird is good. Get her food.* The words were faint, but hopefully Mina would figure out what happened.

The Abbey children waved at the last camera. Banks checked his watch. They had to leave even if the mice didn't show up soon.

Dr. Abbey led his children to the door.

"They're going!" Ava said.

"Gregory, let's show Zitkala the tunnel," Mrs. Squeakerton said. "Get to the bench, little mice."

Ava and Dean ran to their meeting place. They jumped up and down and waved their arms.

Finally, Macey spotted the mice. She hurried

over. Unfortunately, her dad followed. Parents are so nosy sometimes!

"Did you forget something?" Dr. Abbey asked. "We need to go."

"I know. I know." Macey set her backpack on the ground. She tapped the bench. Ava hurried into the backpack. Dean waited.

"Dean," she hissed. "What are you doing?"

"Waiting for Mom. Macey will leave as soon as I'm in there."

Ava's head hurt. If they ever got back to the White House, she was going to nap for a week.

"I sure hope there's good food on the flight." Dr. Abbey scooped up his daughter's backpack.

"Dad!" Macey cried out.

"What?" Dr. Abbey almost dropped the backpack in surprise.

She grabbed for the backpack. "Please . . . that's my private stuff."

"What do you have in here—gold?" He laughed.

Ava felt like she might throw up.

Macey set the backpack on the ground again and tapped the bench with her foot. Dean glanced at the staff room door. How far was that tunnel anyway?

Finally, Mrs. Squeakerton and Gregory popped their heads through the doorway. Dean waved to them. Dr. Abbey was looking at his phone. Ava and Dean couldn't worry much about Macey seeing their mom and Gregory. The adult mice ran over to the bench.

"Ava's in there," Dean said. "Are you ready?"

They held hands as they slipped into the backpack. The Squeakertons all sighed so loudly they were sure Dr. Abbey could hear it.

Macey smiled at her dad. "Let's go. I miss home."

The Abbeys walked down the trail to the parking lot. The cars in the presidential motorcade would take them to Air Force One.

Ava couldn't wait to give her friend a gift. She tapped Macey on the shoulder.

"What did you find, little mouse?" Macey stood in front of their car, taking in one more view of Mount Rushmore.

Ava held up her souvenir.

"Where on earth did you get a cat brooch?" Macey asked. She turned the brooch around in her hand. "It looks like Clover!"

Ava smiled. This was the best way she could think of to say thank you to her friend.

"Banks, look at this." Macey held up the jewelry in the sunlight.

"Is that real gold?" Banks whistled.

"How did she get this?" Macey asked. "They were gone for one day! This thing did not come from a gift shop. And did you notice? More mice ran into my backpack. The big one that looks like a gerbil was with them. Do you really think they visited family? How do mice in the White House even *talk* to mice in South Dakota?"

Banks threw his arm around his sister. "What did I tell you? Mice are smart."

So true. This might have been the Squeakertons' first mystery, but it wouldn't be their last.

The Presidents of the United States

George Washington
1789–1797

John Adams
1797–1801

Thomas Jefferson
1801–1809

James Madison
1809–1817

James Monroe
1817–1825

John Quincy Adams
1825–1829

Andrew Jackson
1829–1837

Martin Van Buren
1837–1841

William Henry
Harrison
1841

John Tyler
1841–1845

James K. Polk
1845–1849

Zachary Taylor
1849–1850

Millard Fillmore
1850–1853

Franklin Pierce
1853–1857

James Buchanan
1857–1861

Abraham Lincoln
1861–1865

Andrew Johnson
1865–1869

Ulysses S. Grant
1869–1877

Rutherford B. Hayes
1877–1881

James Garfield
1881

Chester A. Arthur
1881–1885

Grover Cleveland
1885–1889

Benjamin Harrison
1889–1893

Grover Cleveland
1893–1897

William McKinley
1897–1901

Theodore Roosevelt
1901–1909

William Howard Taft
1909–1913

Woodrow Wilson
1913–1921

Warren G. Harding
1921–1923

Calvin Coolidge
1923–1929

Herbert Hoover
1929–1933

Franklin D. Roosevelt
1933–1945

Harry S. Truman
1945–1953

Dwight D.
Eisenhower
1953–1961

John F. Kennedy
1961–1963

Lyndon B. Johnson
1963–1969

Richard M. Nixon
1969–1974

Gerald R. Ford
1974–1977

James "Jimmy"
Carter
1977–1981

Ronald Reagan
1981–1989

George H. W. Bush
1989–1993

William J. "Bill"
Clinton
1993–2001

George W. Bush
2001–2009

Barack Obama
2009–2017

Donald J. Trump
2017–

Mount Rushmore

Mount Rushmore is a national memorial. Memorials are structures built in remembrance of people who have died. The idea to carve famous people into the mountain came from South Dakota historian Doane Robinson. He wanted to carve American West heroes like Lewis and Clark, Red Cloud, and Buffalo Bill Cody. The sculptor, Gutzon Borglum, thought four famous presidents would bring more tourists to the Black Hills. He believed these presidents made a significant difference in United States history. The presidents are honored in other ways too: the Washington Monument, the Lincoln Memorial, the Thomas Jefferson Memorial, and Theodore Roosevelt National Park.

Mice Are Smart!
Four Totally Fun Facts
About Mount Rushmore

1. The faces of Mount Rushmore are sixty feet high. That's as tall as a six-story building!

2. George Washington's nose is the longest! Our first president's nose is twenty-one feet long, while the other presidential noses are twenty feet.

3. The eyes of each president are eleven feet wide, and their mouths are approximately eighteen feet wide.

4. Though the workers had to climb 700 stairs every day and work was dangerous, no one died during the carving of Mount Rushmore.

These guys are really the BIG cheese!

The Lakota Sioux: The Original Occupants

Many American Indians disagree with the carving of Mount Rushmore, a mountain they called the Six Grandfathers. Rushmore is part of the Paha Sapa, or the Black Hills, which is sacred land to the Lakota Sioux. In 1868, the US government signed a treaty with the Sioux people promising the Black Hills to the Great Sioux Reservation. Gold was soon found, and the government took back the land and ignored the treaty.

American Indians have tried to preserve their culture. Chief Henry Standing Bear invited sculptor Korczak Ziolkowski to carve the Crazy Horse Memorial. This Black Hills statue of the great Sioux chief has been under construction since 1948.

In 2004, an American Indian, Gerard Baker, became superintendent of Mount Rushmore. He introduced American Indian culture to the park's daily activities and exhibits.

Theodore Roosevelt: Not Just a Pretty (Stone) Face

Theodore Roosevelt first visited North Dakota in 1883. It was during this time that Theodore saw how our country's resources were being ruined. Land was destroyed, and animals and vegetation died out.

When he became president, Theodore Roosevelt decided to conserve our beautiful wildlife and public lands. He created the Forest Service. He passed a law that established national monuments. During his time as president, five national parks were dedicated. He helped to protect around 230 million acres of land!

Today, you can take your family on a great American road trip! Turn the page to see a map of just a few of the amazing monuments and national parks you can visit in the great U.S. of A.!

Real men protect the earth!

Mount St. Helens National Volcanic Monument (Washington)

Devils Tower National Monument (Wyoming)

Wind Cave National Park (South Dakota)

WA

MT

ND

OR

ID

SD

WY

NE

Yosemite National Park (California)

NV

UT

CO

Bryce Canyon National Park (Utah)

CA

AZ

NM

Grand Canyon National Park (Arizona)

Great Sand Dunes National Park and Preserve (Colorado)

AK

HI

Glacier Bay National Park and Preserve (Alaska)

World War II Valor in the Pacific National Monument (Hawaii)

White Sands National Monument (New Mexico)

TX

Agate Fossil Beds
National Monument
(Nebraska)

Voyageurs National Park
(Minnesota)

Cuyahoga Valley
National Park (Ohio)

VT NH ME

MN

WI

MI

NY

MA

RI

CT

IA

PA

NJ

Statue of
Liberty
National
Monument
(New York)

IL

IN

OH

DE

MD

MO

WV

VA

KY

NC

Great Smoky
Mountains
National Park
(Tennessee–North
Carolina border)

TN

AR

SC

MS

AL

GA

Fort Sumter
National Monument
(South Carolina)

LA

FL

Birmingham Civil
Rights National
Monument
(Alabama)

Mammoth Cave
National Park
(Kentucky)

Everglades National Park
(Florida)

Learn to Draw Ava and Dean!

Follow the steps below to draw Ava and Dean.

Step 1: Draw rectangles for their bodies and triangles for their heads.

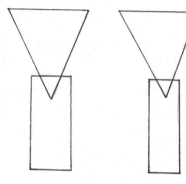

Step 2: Add circles for their ears. Then draw small rectangles for their arms and legs.

Step 3: Add a triangle to the side of each head to help make a mouse-shaped snout and add a triangle to be the tip of the nose. Then add circles to make eyes and hands. For Ava, add triangles to make the shape of her skirt.

Step 4: Now that you have the shape in place, start adding curves to your drawing to make it look smoother. Then add details like whiskers, mouse packs, buttons, and more!